Favorite
Fairy Tales

PaRragon

Bath · New York · Singapore · Hong Kong · Cologne · Delhi
Melbourne · Amsterdam · Johannesburg · Auckland · Shenzhen

First published by Parragon in 2011

Parragon
Queen Street House
4 Queen Street
Bath BA1 1HE, UK

ISBN 978-1-4454-4113-9

Printed in Indonesia

Contents

The Gingerbread Man

Once upon a time, a little old man and a little old woman lived in a cottage near the river.

One morning, the little old man and the little old woman were feeling hungry, so the little old woman decided to bake a gingerbread man.

The little old woman mixed together the flour, sugar, butter, corn syrup, ginger, baking soda, and egg to make the gingerbread dough.

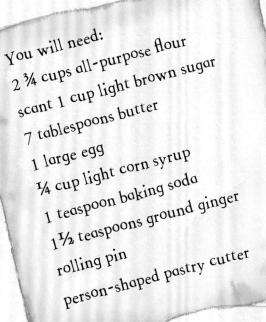

You will need:
2 ¾ cups all-purpose flour
scant 1 cup light brown sugar
7 tablespoons butter
1 large egg
¼ cup light corn syrup
1 teaspoon baking soda
1½ teaspoons ground ginger
rolling pin
person-shaped pastry cutter

Then she rolled the mixture out flat and used the cutter to make it into the shape of a gingerbread man.

Finally, she made some icing for his eyes, mouth, and nose, and she gave him three currant buttons.

At last, the gingerbread man was ready to be baked and the little old woman put him into the oven.

Half an hour later, the little old woman opened the oven door and took out the baking sheet, where the gingerbread man lay, golden and crisp.

Suddenly, the gingerbread man jumped off the baking sheet and ran through the kitchen.

"Stop!" cried the old woman, running after him. "Come back. I want to eat you."

But the gingerbread man didn't want to be eaten, and he was too fast for the little old woman.

"Run, run as fast as you can. You can't catch me, I'm the gingerbread man!" he chanted.

The gingerbread man ran into the garden
and passed the little old man.

"Stop!" cried the little old man, setting down
his wheelbarrow. "I want to eat you."

But the gingerbread man ran even faster.

"I've run away from a little old woman and
I can run away from you," he said.

"Run, run as fast
as you can.

You can't catch me,

I'm the gingerbread man!"
he chanted.

The little old man and the little
old woman chased the gingerbread
man, but he was too fast.

The gingerbread man ran
through the yard and passed a pig.

"Stop," snorted the pig.
"I want to eat you."

But the gingerbread man ran even faster.

"I've run away from a little old
woman and a little old man, and
I can run away from you," he said.

"Run, run as fast as you can. You can't catch me, I'm the gingerbread man!" he chanted.

The little pig chased the gingerbread man, followed by the little old man and the little old woman.

But the gingerbread man was too fast.

The gingerbread man passed a cow by the barn.

"Stop," mooed the cow. "I want to eat you."

But the gingerbread man ran even faster.

"I've run away from a little old woman, a little old man, and a pig, and I can run away from you," he said.

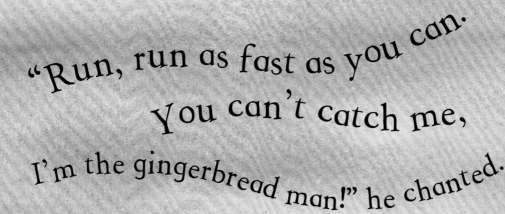

"Run, run as fast as you can.
You can't catch me,
I'm the gingerbread man!" he chanted.

The cow, the pig, the little old man,
and the little old woman all chased
after the gingerbread man. But the
gingerbread man was too fast.

The gingerbread man passed a horse in the field.

"Stop," neighed the horse. "I want to eat you."

But the gingerbread man ran even faster.

"I've run away from a little old woman, a little old man, a pig, and a cow, and I can run away from you," he said.

"Run, run as fast as you can.
You can't catch me,
I'm the gingerbread man!" he chanted.

The horse chased
the gingerbread man,
followed by ...

the cow ...

the pig ...

the little old man ...

and the little
old woman.

But the gingerbread
man was too fast.

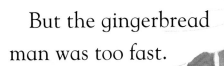

Then the gingerbread man reached
a river and stopped.

The sparkly water whirled and swirled in front
of him as his reflection danced along the ripples.

The gingerbread man shuddered.

"Oh, no! I can't swim," he cried.
"How will I get across?"

A sly and hungry fox was waiting nearby.

He saw the gingerbread man and licked his lips.

"Jump onto my tail and I will take you across the river," he said.

So the gingerbread man jumped onto the fox's tail and the fox swam across the river.

After swimming halfway, the fox spoke
to the gingerbread man.

"You're too heavy for my tail, jump
onto my back," he said.

So the gingerbread man ran lightly
down the fox's bushy tail and jumped onto
his back, holding tightly onto his fur.

After a while, the fox cried, "You're too heavy for my back. Jump onto my nose."

And the gingerbread man sprinted down the fox's back and jumped onto his nose.

But as soon as they reached the riverbank, the fox flipped the gingerbread man high up into the air, **snapped** his mouth shut, and **gobbled** him up.

And that was the end of the gingerbread man!

The End

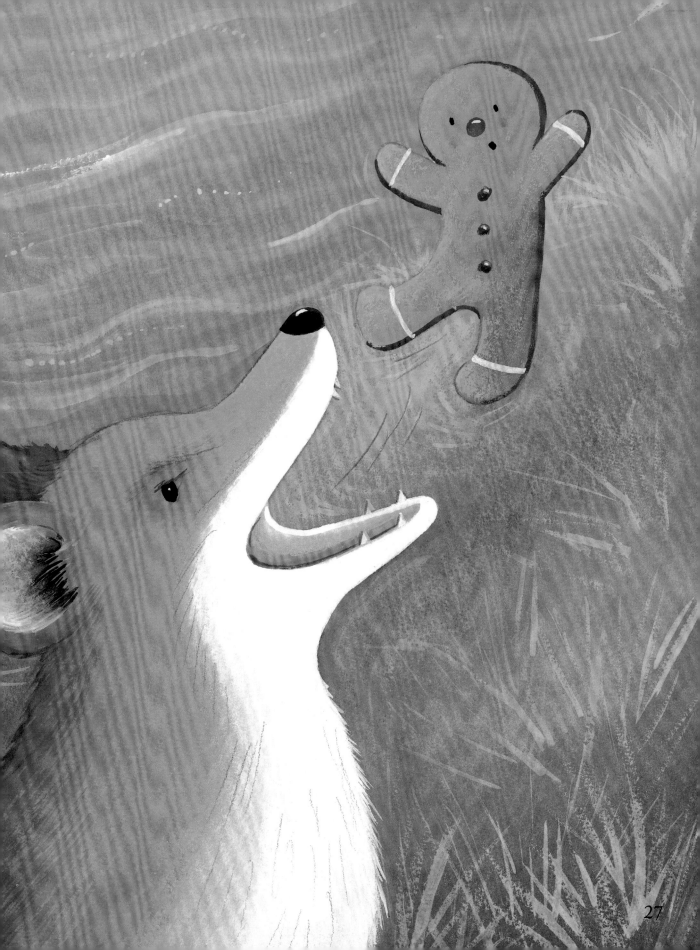

Cinderella

Once upon a time, there was a kind, sweet girl called Cinderella. Her mother died when she was very young, and her father married again, but his new wife was mean and bossy.

Her two daughters, Anastasia and Drusilla, were as mean and nasty as their mother. They treated Cinderella like a servant.

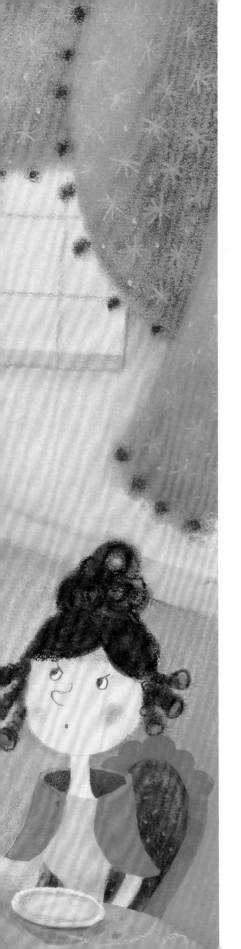

One morning, Cinderella was busy polishing her stepsisters' shoes, when there was a knock at the door.

"What are you waiting for?" snapped Drusilla. "Answer it!"

Cinderella opened the door to find a smart footman. He handed her a gold envelope and made a graceful bow.

"The palace is holding a ball for the Prince's birthday tonight," he announced. "Every girl in the kingdom is invited."

You are invited to the Prince's birthday ball.

"It's not meant for YOU!" cried Anastasia, snatching the invitation.

"But the footman said that every girl is invited," protested Cinderella's father.

"Of course she may go," said Cinderella's stepmother, slyly, "as long as she has finished all her chores ..."

Cinderella was thrilled. "I'll start my jobs right away!"

But no matter how hard Cinderella worked, her list of jobs just kept growing. Her stepsisters and stepmother saw to that.

"Iron my dress!"

"Brush my hair!"

"Paint my nails!"

"Fetch my necklace!"

"Oh dear!" giggled the stepsisters, when
the coach arrived to take them to the palace,
"aren't you ready yet?" And they flounced out,
laughing unkindly.

Poor Cinderella sat by the fireside and big tears rolled down her cheeks.

"I wish I could wear a pretty dress and meet the Prince!" she sighed.

"Wishes can come true!" whispered a voice.

Suddenly, the room was filled with sparkling light as a fairy appeared.

"Dry your eyes, Cinderella," said the fairy. "I am your Fairy Godmother—and we have work to do!"

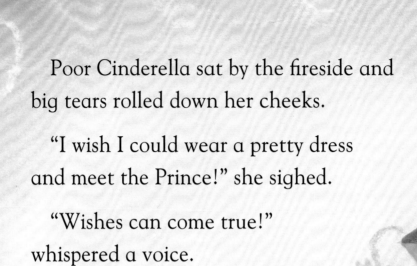

"Go to the garden and fetch me the biggest pumpkin you can find," her Fairy Godmother said.

Cinderella was puzzled, but she did as she was told.

SWOOSH!

With a wave of her wand, Cinderella's Fairy Godmother transformed the pumpkin into a beautiful coach.

Next, the Fairy Godmother searched around the courtyard and rounded up four white mice and a rat.

SWOOSH!

Four gleaming white horses and a smart coachman appeared.

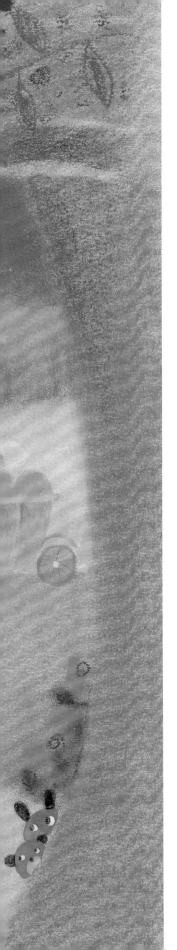

"That's that. Now for you," said the Fairy Godmother.

SWOOSH!

In a burst of twinkling stars, Cinderella's plain dress was transformed into waves of soft silk, and on her feet were two dainty crystal slippers.

"I feel like a princess," gasped Cinderella, stepping into the coach.

"You look like a princess," smiled her Fairy Godmother. "But remember, my magic won't last. On the final stroke of twelve, everything you see before you will disappear."

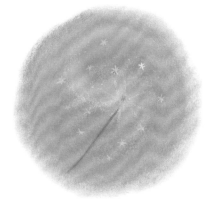

When Cinderella entered the ballroom, a murmur rippled around the room. "She must be a princess!" whispered the guests. They couldn't take their eyes off the beautiful girl—and neither could the Prince. He rushed over and asked her to dance.

All night long, Cinderella and the Prince
twirled around the dance floor. Anastasia and
Drusilla watched grumpily from the side.

43

Suddenly, the palace clock began to strike.
BONG! BONG! Cinderella remembered the
warning. The magic was about to end!

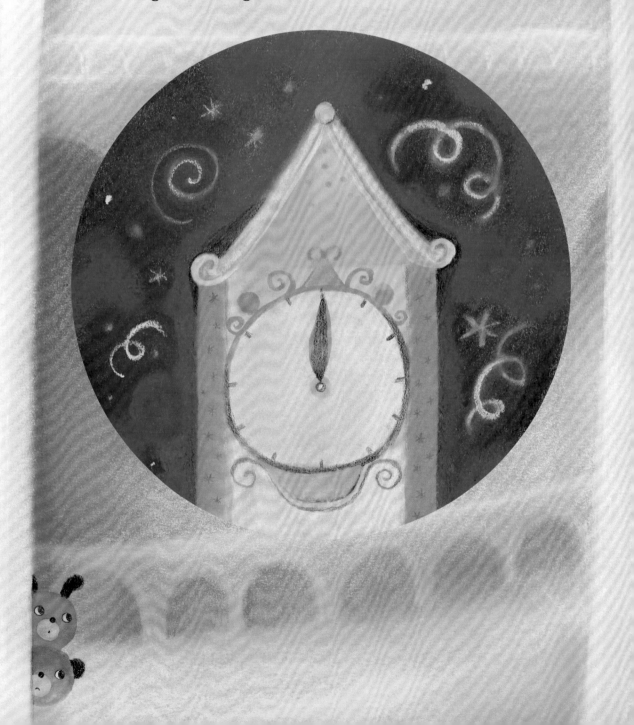

"I'm sorry!" she cried. "I have to go ..."

The Prince chased after her, but he was too late. All that remained was a glass slipper, twinkling in the moonlight.

The following morning,
the Prince set out to find the
beautiful girl from the ball.

"Every girl in the land must
try the slipper," he said.

Girl after girl tried to squeeze
her foot into the tiny shoe, but
with no success. Finally, the
Prince arrived at Cinderella's
house.

Anastasia and Drusilla fought
over the glass slipper. But no
matter how much they squashed
and squeezed, they could not
force their big feet into the
dainty shoe.

"Is there no one else?" asked the Prince.

"There is Cinderella," said her father, bravely.

"Let her try," said the Prince, kneeling to slip the shoe onto Cinderella's pretty foot.

"It fits!" he cried happily. "My search is over! Will you marry me?"

Cinderella agreed at once.

"But she can't!" shrieked her furious stepmother. "She didn't even go to the ball!"

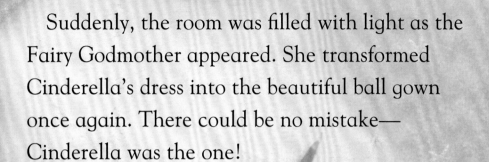

Suddenly, the room was filled with light as the
Fairy Godmother appeared. She transformed
Cinderella's dress into the beautiful ball gown
once again. There could be no mistake—
Cinderella was the one!

The wedding took place the very next day.

"And this time, you don't just look like
a princess!" whispered her Fairy Godmother.
"You really are one!"

The Prince and Cinderella lived happily
ever after in the palace.

Meanwhile, Anastasia and
Drusilla had to polish their
own shoes and iron their own
dresses—and that made them
grumpier than ever!

A yumm

Goldilocks and the Three Bears

Once upon a time, Goldilocks was playing in the wood near her home.

Her blonde curls bounced and bobbed as she danced around the rustling trees and skipped along the pebbly path, humming to herself.

Suddenly, Goldilocks stopped and sniffed the air ...

...a delicious smell was coming from the middle of the wood.

53

RUMBLE RUMBLE!

Goldilocks' tummy grumbled loudly.

Goldilocks followed the delicious smell and soon found herself in front of a little house.

"How sweet," she cried, clapping her hands in delight. "I wonder who lives here ..."

Goldilocks knocked loudly on the front door.

KNOCK, KNOCK, KNO ...

But on the last KNOCK, the door swung open.
Nobody was home.

Goldilocks saw three bowls of porridge on the
kitchen table. Her tummy rumbled again.

"I'm sure no one will mind if
I go inside and have a little
taste of this porridge,"
she told herself.

Goldilocks picked up a spoon and started to eat from the biggest bowl of porridge.

"Yuck!" she cried, shaking her golden hair. "This porridge is far too cold!"

Goldilocks tried the medium-size bowl.

"Ouch!" she gasped. "This porridge is far too hot!"

There was still the small bowl to try. Goldilocks took a little mouthful.

"Mmmm!" she sighed, licking her lips. "This porridge is perfect!"

And she ate it all up.

Then, Goldilocks went into the living room for a rest. She saw a big chair, a medium-size chair and a tiny, little chair.

Goldilocks climbed onto the biggest chair, but she felt too high up.

"This chair is too big!" she said.

Next, Goldilocks clambered onto the medium-size chair. But she sank so far into the squashy cushions that she struggled to get back out.

"This chair is too soft!" she cried.

Then, Goldilocks tried the tiny chair.

"This chair is perfect!" beamed Goldilocks. She was wriggling and jiggling around to get even more comfortable, when …

CR-R-R-RACK!

The chair broke into little pieces.

"Oh, no!" Goldilocks gasped. "Maybe I'll find somewhere to lie down instead."

Upstairs, Goldilocks found three beds.

There was a big bed, a medium-size bed and a tiny, little bed.

Goldilocks jumped up and down on each bed in turn.

The big bed was too hard, the medium-size bed was too soft, and the little bed was …

"Perfect!" Goldilocks sighed happily.

And the little girl crawled under the covers and fell fast asleep.

ZzzzzZZzzzzzz

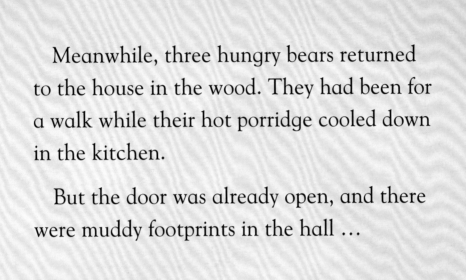

Meanwhile, three hungry bears returned to the house in the wood. They had been for a walk while their hot porridge cooled down in the kitchen.

But the door was already open, and there were muddy footprints in the hall …

Daddy Bear gasped and gave out a loud

ROAR!

"Someone's been
eating my porridge!"
he growled.

"Someone's been eating my porridge,
too," bellowed Mommy Bear.

"Someone's been
eating my porridge,"
squeaked Baby Bear,
"and gobbled it all up!"

Then the three bears padded into the living room.

"Someone's been sitting in my chair!" roared Daddy Bear, looking at a strand of golden hair on the armrest.

"Someone's been sitting in my chair, too," growled Mommy Bear, peering at the crease in the cushion.

"Someone's been sitting in my chair," yelped Baby Bear, "and broken it!"

Suddenly, the three bears heard a noise coming from upstairs ...

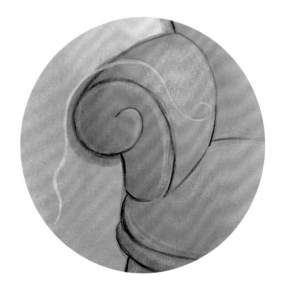

zzzzzzzzzzzzzzzzzzzzzzzzzzzz

71

Daddy Bear, Mommy Bear and Baby Bear
rushed up the stairs and into the bedroom.

"Someone's been sleeping in
my bed!" roared Daddy Bear,
looking at the crumpled sheets.

"Someone's been sleeping in my bed, too," growled
Mommy Bear, straightening the untidy covers.

ZZZZZZZZZZZZZZZZZZZZZ

"Someone's been sleeping
in my bed," squeaked Baby
Bear, pointing to Goldilocks,
"and she's still there!"

Goldilocks woke up with a start and found three bears peering down at her.

She leaped out of bed, ran out of the house, and sped off through the forest as fast as her legs would carry her.

And the three bears never saw Goldilocks again.

Little Red Riding Hood

Once upon a time, there was a little girl who lived with her mommy in a house on the edge of a big forest.

Whenever the little girl went outside to play, she wore a beautiful red cape that her grandma had made especially for her.

The cape was nice and warm, and kept the little girl cozy on cold days. It had a big, red hood, so everyone called the little girl **Little Red Riding Hood.**

One day, Little Red Riding Hood's mommy asked her to take a basket of food to Grandma.

"Grandma isn't feeling well," Mommy explained, "and I'm sure she'd love to see you."

Little Red Riding Hood didn't see Grandma very often because she lived on the other side of the forest. She helped Mommy draw a map on a piece of paper so she wouldn't get lost. Then she slid the map inside a pocket in her cape.

"Now hurry along," said Mommy, helping Little Red
Riding Hood into the cape. "And remember, don't
talk to any strangers along the way."

Little Red Riding Hood took the basket of food and
waved good bye to her mommy.

"I won't," she said, skipping into the forest.

On the way, Little Red Riding Hood saw some beautiful blue flowers.

"Grandma might like these," she thought, bending down to pick a handful.

Little Red Riding Hood was so busy choosing flowers, she didn't realize she was no longer alone in the forest ...

"Hello, little girl,"

said a deep, growly voice.

Little Red Riding Hood jumped
with fright.

81

A big wolf peered out from behind one of the trees and grinned at Little Red Riding Hood.

"Oh, hello," replied Little Red Riding Hood, smiling back at the wolf. She had already forgotten her mommy's warning.

"Where are you going?" growled the wolf.

"I'm visiting my sick grandma who lives on the other side of the forest," Little Red Riding Hood explained. "I'm picking some pretty flowers to take with me."

"Ah, what a kind girl you are," smiled the wolf, showing off his razor-sharp teeth. "Your grandma is very lucky to have such a sweet and thoughtful granddaughter."

Just then the wolf's belly gave a LOUD, rumbly grumble.

"What was that?" asked Little Red Riding Hood, peering up at the wolf.

"Just some thunder over the hills," said the sneaky wolf, trying his best not to lick his greedy lips.

Then the wolf ran as fast as he could to Grandma's house.

The hungry wolf peered through Grandma's window and saw the old lady in bed.

With one big, bloodcurdling howl, the wolf dashed through the front door, ran into the bedroom, and gobbled up Grandma in one large GULP!

Then the wolf put on Grandma's spare nightcap and glasses, clambered into her bed, and pulled the quilt up to his chin.

Now all he had to do
was wait for Little Red
Riding Hood to arrive.

When Little Red Riding Hood finally reached the house, the little girl was surprised to find the front door wide open.

"Hello," she called. "Are you there, Grandma?"

"I'm in the bedroom," called the wolf in a strange, wobbly voice.

"Oh," thought Little Red Riding Hood. "Grandma does sound odd. She must be very sick indeed."

Little Red Riding Hood went into the bedroom and gasped in surprise when she saw her grandma. She looked sort of ... different.

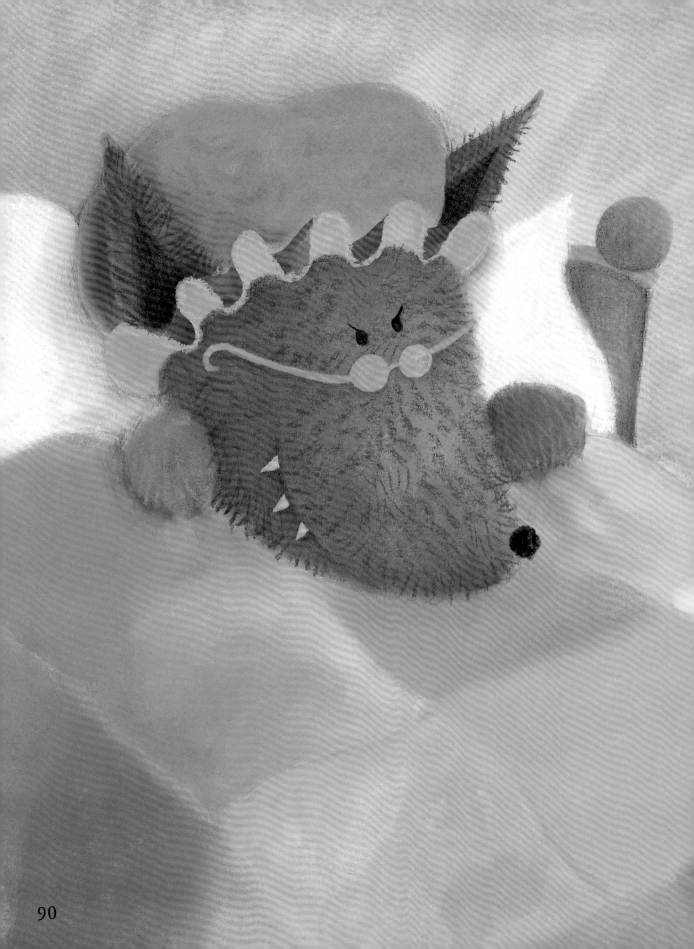

90

Little Red Riding Hood hoped that whatever it was that Grandma had, it wasn't catching!

"My, what big eyes you've got, Grandma," said Little Red Riding Hood.

"All the better for seeing you with, my dear" the wolf replied, in his wobbly voice.

"And what big ears you've got, Grandma," Little Red Riding Hood added, moving closer.

"All the better for hearing you with, my dear," said the wolf, giving Little Red Riding Hood his toothiest grin.

"M ... m ... my, what big teeth you've got, Grandma,"

stuttered Little Red Riding Hood in a very shaky voice.

"ALL THE BETTER FOR EATING YOU WITH!"

93

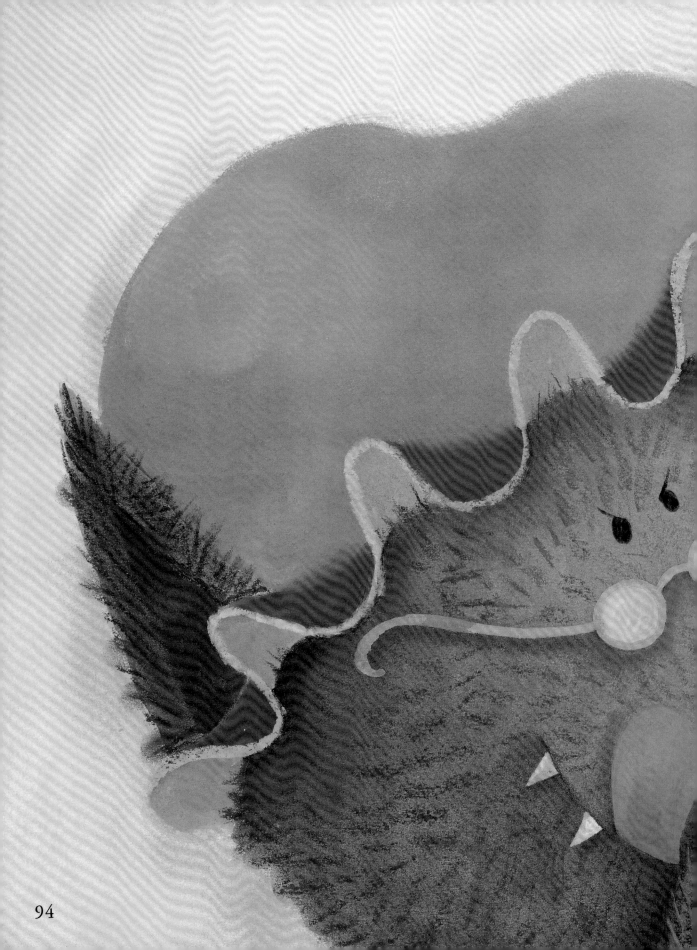

Little Red Riding Hood SCREAMED and tried to run away. But it was no good. The hungry wolf was too fast.

He leaped out of the bed and gobbled her up in a single, greedy GULP!

A passing lumberjack heard Little Red Riding Hood's scream and ran into the house.

When he saw the wolf's enormous belly, he guessed what had happened. He picked up the wolf and shook him as hard as he could.

The wolf's mouth gaped open, and out flew Little Red Riding Hood, closely followed by Grandma.

Grandma and Litt

Red Riding Hood weren't hurt, but they were VERY angry!

Grandma chased the wolf out of the bedroom, through the cottage, into the forest, and over the hill.

The lumberjack and Little Red Riding Hood followed closely behind.

Soon, the wolf was gone forever, and ...

Little Red Riding Hood never

spoke to strangers again.

The End

Snow White

One snowy winter's day, a queen sat sewing by her window.

She accidentally pricked her finger with the needle—ouch!—and three drops of blood fell on the snow.

The Queen looked at the bright red blood on the white snow, against the black wood of the window frame, and thought: "I wish I had a child with lips as red as blood, skin as white as snow, and hair as black as ebony wood!"

Some time after that, the Queen gave birth to a little girl with deep red lips, snowy-white skin, and glossy hair as black as ebony. She called her **Snow White.**

Sadly, the Queen died, and the King married again. His new wife was beautiful, but cruel and selfish. She had a magic mirror, and every day she looked into it and said:

"Mirror, mirror, on the wall, Who is the fairest one of all?"

And every day the mirror replied,

"You, O Queen, are the fairest of all."

But as Snow White grew up, she grew more beautiful. And so, one morning, the Queen's mirror said to her:

"You, O Queen, are fair, it's true. But Snow White is much fairer than you!"

In a jealous rage, the Queen called her huntsman.

"I never want to see Snow White's face again," she told him. "Take her into the forest and kill her."

The huntsman took Snow White to
the edge of the forest—but he could
not bear to hurt her.

"Run away, child," he said.
"Don't ever come back, or
the Queen will kill you."

Poor, scared Snow White! She
was all alone, lost in the forest,
running for her life.

Toward nightfall, Snow White came to a little house deep in the forest. She knocked softly, but there was no answer, so she let herself in.

Inside, Snow White found a table and seven, tiny chairs. Upstairs there were seven, little beds.

"I'm so tired," she yawned, and she lay down and fell fast asleep.

A while later, she woke with a start. Seven, little men were standing round her bed.

"Who are you?" she asked.

"We are the seven dwarfs who live here," said one of the little men. "We work in the mines all day. Who are YOU?"

"I am Snow White," she replied, and she told them her sad story.

The dwarfs felt sorry for Snow White, and they wanted to help.

"If you will cook and clean for us," said the eldest dwarf, "you can stay here, and we will keep you safe."

Snow White gratefully agreed, and began that very evening by cooking the dwarfs a pot of tasty, hot soup for their supper.

When they left for work the next morning, the dwarfs made Snow White promise not to go out, or open the door, or speak to anyone.

Meanwhile, the Queen was back at her magic mirror. But she was shocked by what it told her:

"You are the fairest here, it's true,
But there is someone fairer than you.
Deep in the forest, in a cozy den,
Snow White lives with
seven, little men."

"What?" shrieked the Queen. "Snow White is ALIVE?"

In a wild frenzy, she raced to her secret chamber, in the darkest depths of the castle.

There, the Queen, who was really a wicked witch, brewed a deadly potion and poisoned a rosy, red apple.

Disguising herself as an old pedlar woman, she set out for the seven dwarfs' cottage.

Snow White was busy in the kitchen when she heard a tapping on the window. She looked up to see an old woman peering in.

"Apples for sale," the old woman croaked. "Try my lovely, red apples!" And she handed the poisoned apple to Snow White.

Snow White couldn't resist. She took a big bite …

… and

fell

down

motionless.

The Queen cackled with delight and hurried home to her magic mirror. At last it gave her the answer she wanted:

"You, O Queen, are the fairest of all!"

The dwarfs wept bitterly when they came home to find their lovely Snow White lying totally still on the floor.

They carefully laid her in a glass case and watched over her, day and night.

One day, a prince came riding through the forest. When he saw the beautiful girl in the glass case, he instantly fell in love with her.

"Please let me take her back to my castle," he begged the dwarfs, and they agreed.

As the dwarfs helped to lift the case, one of them stumbled, and the piece of apple that was stuck in Snow White's throat came loose. Snow White coughed, and her eyes flew open.

"Where am I?" she gasped.

"You are with someone who loves you more than life itself," said the Prince. "Please marry me."

Snow White looked into the Prince's kind, gentle eyes, and knew she loved him, too. "Yes," she said. "I will."

And so they were married, with the dwarfs beside them. They all lived happily together in the Prince's castle for the rest of their long lives.

Sleeping Beauty

Once upon a time, in a faraway land, a king and queen lived in a grand castle. They were very content, but they longed for a child. So, imagine how happy they were when the Queen gave birth to a beautiful baby girl.

"Let's have a party to celebrate," the King beamed.

"Oh, yes!" agreed the Queen.

You are invited to a party at the palace on the first day of spring to celebrate the birth of our baby girl. From the King and Queen.

The day of the party arrived. Tables were laden with delicious food and there was music and dancing in the great hall. One by one, the guests placed their presents beside the Princess's cradle. Last of all, the four good fairies presented their gifts in a shower of fairy dust.

"You will be incredibly clever," said Whim.

"You will be a wonderful dancer," said Whirl.

"You will be a fabulous singer," said Whistle.

But before Wisp, the fourth good fairy, could speak, there was a flash of lightning, followed by a wicked cackle.

HA! HA! HA!

A hush fell over the great hall. It was Wheedle, the wicked fairy. The King had forgotten to send her an invitation—and she was furious!

She flew up to the cradle and waved her evil wand over the Princess's head. "Here's my gift," she shrieked. "One day, the Princess will prick her finger on a spindle and die." Then she disappeared in a puff of black smoke.

Everyone gasped. The Queen sobbed and
the King shouted for the guards to burn
every spinning wheel and spindle in the land.

Then Wisp fluttered over.

"I cannot break the spell,"
she said, "but I can change it.
If the Princess does prick her finger,
she will not die. She will fall into a deep
sleep and will one day be woken by
the kiss of true love."

The years passed and
the Princess grew up to be
everything the good fairies
had promised.

Then
one day,
the Princess
was exploring
the castle, when she
came across a tower
she had never
seen before.

She climbed the steep
steps and entered a tiny
room. There, in the
corner, was a
long-forgotten
spinning wheel.

Ouch!

The Princess had never seen anything
like it. She brushed off the cobwebs and pricked
her finger. She instantly fell into a deep sleep.

And that is how the King and Queen found her. The good fairies tried to help, but there was nothing they could do to wake the Princess. They laid her on a bed, and then the fairies cast a gentle spell over the whole castle. Everyone from the King to the cook's cat fell into a deep sleep.

135

A hundred years rolled by and a giant hedge of thorns grew up around the castle. Many tried to cut their way through the thorns, but all failed. Then one day, a handsome prince came riding by. When he saw the tower poking up from the forest of thorns, he became very curious.

He drew out his sword to hack his way through, but somehow a path magically appeared before him.

ZZzzzzZZZzzzzzZZZzzzz

At last the Prince came to the castle. He walked past the snoring guards at the gate, and stopped to admire the smart horses dozing in the stables. He almost tripped over the cook slumped beside her cooking pot, and he bowed before the King and Queen sleeping on their thrones. Then, as if in a trance, he was drawn up the steps of the tower.

As soon as the Prince set eyes upon the Princess,
his heart leaped. He had never seen anyone so lovely.
He bent down and kissed her gently on the lips.

The Princess opened her eyes and smiled.
"I've had such a lovely sleep," she sighed.

As she spoke the words, everyone in the castle woke up and went about their tasks as if nothing had happened. The guards stood to attention, the groom continued brushing the horses, and the cook stirred her cooking pot.

The King and Queen were delighted. Not only had the handsome Prince broken the wicked spell, but he was in love with their beautiful daughter.

"Excellent!" bellowed the King. "Let's have a royal wedding!"

The Prince and Princess were soon married and the King threw a fabulous party. Everyone was invited—except the wicked fairy.

Luckily, this time the good fairies cast a spell to make sure she stayed away.

After the wedding, the Prince and Princess rode off on the Prince's fine horse and lived happily ever after.

The End

Hansel and Gretel

Hansel and Gretel lived by the forest with their stepmother and their father, who was a poor woodcutter.

One evening, the family had nothing to eat but a few crusts of bread. Hansel and Gretel went to bed feeling hungry. As they lay there, they heard their stepmother and father talking.

"There are too many mouths to feed," said their stepmother. "We must take your children into the forest and leave them there."

"Never!" cried their father.

"Well, I'm not going to starve," their stepmother barked. "The children are going, and that is that!"

Gretel began to cry, but Hansel comforted her. "Don't worry. I'll think of something," he promised.

The next morning, Hansel and Gretel's stepmother woke the children at daybreak.

"Get up!" she ordered. "We're going into the forest to chop wood."

She gave Hansel and Gretel a crust of bread each for their lunch.

Hansel broke his bread into tiny pieces in
his pocket and, as they walked along ...

... he secretly dropped a trail of crumbs on the ground.

Deep in the forest, Hansel and Gretel's father built them a fire.

"Your stepmother and I are going to chop wood now," he said. "We'll return for you at sunset."

After a while, the children shared Gretel's bread and then they curled up at the foot of an old oak tree and fell asleep.

When Hansel and Gretel woke up, it was dark and their little fire had gone out.

"I want to go home," Gretel whimpered.

"Don't worry," said Hansel. "We'll just follow the trail of bread crumbs I left."

But the bread crumbs were gone! The forest birds had eaten them all up.

"We'll wait until morning," Hansel said. "When it's light, we'll find our way home."

HOOT, HOOT!

153

The next morning, the
children were woken by
the sound of birds singing.

In the tree above them, a
snow-white bird flapped its
wings as if to beckon them.

"Look!" cried Hansel. "Maybe
that bird will lead us home!"

But the white bird led them
deeper
into
the
forest ...
... to a little house made of gingerbread!

155

The roof was dripping with sugary icing, the windows were framed with candy canes, and the yard was filled with colorful lollipops.

Delighted, the hungry children began to feast upon the candies.

Suddenly, the door creaked open ...

CR-R-REAK!

... and a croaky voice came from inside.

"Nibble, nibble, like a mouse, who is nibbling at my house?"

An old woman hobbled out, leaning on a crooked stick.

"I can't see very well—who are you?" she asked.

"Just two hungry children," Hansel replied.

"Ah," said the old woman, "well you'd better come inside and I will make you a proper meal."

The old woman placed a plate before Hansel and Gretel, piled high with delicious pancakes. They ate and ate until they were ready to burst!

Then she showed them to two little beds. Hansel and Gretel snuggled down under the soft blankets and fell fast asleep.

But Hansel and Gretel didn't know that the kind old woman was really a wicked witch.

As she watched them sleep, she cackled, "I'll soon fatten these two up. Then they will make a proper meal for ME!"

161

The following morning, the witch dragged Hansel from his bed and threw him into a cage. Then she made Gretel cook her brother a big breakfast.

"Your brother is too skinny," the witch told Gretel. "I'll keep him locked up until he is nice and plump ...

... and then I'll EAT HIM UP!"

Over the next few days, Hansel ate as much food as he could. And every morning, the witch made him stick out his finger so she could feel whether he was fat enough to eat.

But Hansel was clever. He knew the old witch could hardly see, so he stuck a chicken bone through the cage instead.

"Still too scrawny," the witch would say.

One day, the witch grew tired of waiting.

"Whether he be fatter or thinner,
I'll have Hansel for my dinner!"

she crowed.

"Light the oven!" the witch ordered Gretel. "Now crawl in and see whether it's hot enough."

Gretel knew the witch was planning to cook her as well. So she decided to trick the witch.

"The oven's much too small for me," she said.

"Even I could fit inside that oven. Look!" said the witch, sticking her head inside.

The witch let out a big Yeeee-ooooooowwww as Gretel pushed her into the oven and slammed the door shut.

Gretel freed Hansel from his cage, and they danced happily around the kitchen.

"We're safe! We're safe!" they sang.

When the children looked around the witch's house, they found chests crammed with gold and sparkling jewels. They filled their pockets before they set off for home.

Back in the woods, the white bird beckoned to them again. This time, it led them straight home, where their delighted father greeted them with hugs and kisses.

He told them that their cruel stepmother had died, so they had nothing to fear. Hansel and Gretel showed him the treasure they had found.

"We will never go hungry again!" he said.

They all lived happily
ever after. And the white
bird sat on their rooftop and
sang for them every day.

The Three Little Pigs

Once upon a time, there were three little pigs who lived in a cozy house on the hill.

Every day, their mother made them delicious food to eat. But the more the three little pigs ate, the hungrier they got, and the hungrier they got, the more they ate.

It wasn't long before the three little pigs had grown so big that there was no room for them in the cozy house anymore.

"I'm sorry," said their mother one morning, "but it's time you made your own way in the world."

So the very next day, the three little pigs (who were now quite big pigs) left home.

"Always remember to wash behind your ears," called their mother, as she waved good-bye. "And don't forget to watch out for the Big Bad Wolf. He'll eat you for supper, so you'll need to build a big, fine, strong house as quickly as you can to keep him away."

"Don't worry, Ma!" they oinked. "We can look after ourselves!"

And the three little pigs trotted off down the hill, each taking a different path.

It wasn't long before the first little pig met a farmer pulling a cart filled with straw.

"Please may I buy some straw to build a house?" asked the little pig.

"Of course," replied the farmer, "although I can think of better things to build a house with. Why, even the wind could blow down a house of straw!"

But the little pig wasn't listening. He was far too busy stacking straw. A bundle here ... a bundle there ...

There were bundles of straw everywhere!

In no time at all, the house of
straw was finished, and the little
pig went inside for a nap.

He had just shut his eyes, when
there was a knock at the door.

It was the
Big Bad Wolf.

"Little pig, little pig, let me in!" growled the wolf,
licking his lips. He had come for his supper.

"Not by the hair on my chinny-chin-chin!" the little
pig replied.

"Then I'll HUFF ... and I'll PUFF ... and I'll blow your house in!" laughed the wolf. And that's just what he did.

HUFF! PUFF! WHOOSH!

Meanwhile, the second little pig was
walking down the road when he saw
a woodcutter, piling up sticks.

"Please may I buy some?" he asked politely.
"I want to build a house made of sticks."

"Of course," answered the woodcutter,
"although I can think of better things to build a
house with. A house of sticks will soon fall down!"

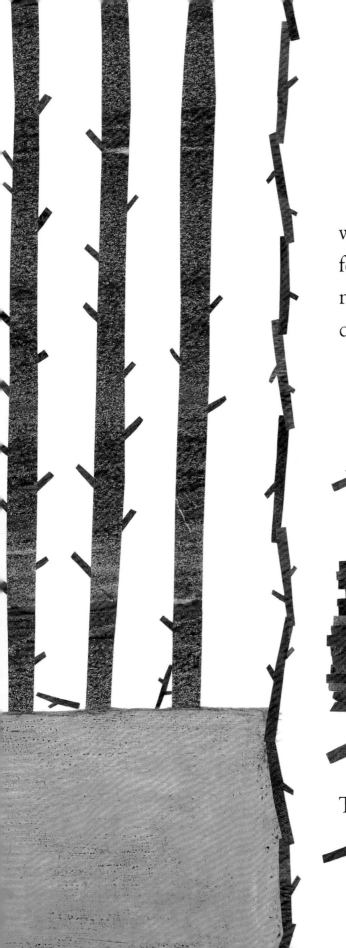

But the second little pig wasn't listening. He was far too busy planning his new home. A stick here … a stick there …

There were sticks everywhere!

Soon the house was finished, and the little pig went inside for a rest. He had just sat down, when there was a knock at the door.

It was the Big Bad Wolf.

"Little pig, little pig, let me in!" he growled hungrily.

"Not by the hair on my chinny-chin-chin!" cried the second little pig, remembering his mother's warning.

"Then I'll HUFF ... and I'll PUFF ... and I'll blow your house in!" cried the wolf. And that's exactly what he did.

HUFF! PUFF! WHOOSH!

Meanwhile, the third little pig met a builder.

"Please can I buy some of your bricks to build my house?" he asked.

"Of course," replied the builder. And he gave the little pig some fine red bricks, along with some roof tiles and a wooden door.

"Don't rush the job," the builder told the little pig. "A fine, strong house of bricks will last forever!"

The third little pig listened well. He would build the strongest house in the land!

All day long, the third little pig worked hard. HEAVE-HO! BANG! BANG! HAMMER! HAMMER! SAW! SAW!

Finally, the house of bricks was finished. And what a fine house it was! It had four strong walls of brick, a tiled roof, a sturdy wooden door, and a large fireplace with a chimney.

The third little pig had just put a pot of turnips on the fire to boil, when all of a sudden he saw his brothers running down the road—closely followed by the Big Bad Wolf.

"Quick!" cried the third little pig, opening the door to let his brothers in. "You can hide in here!"

The wolf, who was very hungry by now,
banged on the sturdy front door.

"Little pigs, little pigs, let me in!" he growled.

The wolf's tummy was rumbling very loudly with hunger.

"Not by the hairs on our chinny-chin-chins!" cried the three little pigs.

"Then I'll HUFF … and I'll PUFF … and I'll blow your house in!" laughed the wolf.

So he HUFFED

and he PUFFED...

and he PUFFED

and he HUFFED...

But the brick house stood firm.

The wolf was furious! He climbed up on
to the roof and shouted down the chimney.
"If I can't blow your house in, I'll come down
the chimney and gobble you all up!"

But little did the wolf know that the pot of turnips
was still bubbling on the fire at the other end.

EEEEEEEYOWWWW!

The Big Bad Wolf landed
in the boiling pot. He leaped
up and ran out of the house,
never to be seen again.

And the three little pigs lived happily
ever after in the house made of bricks.